THIS BOOK BELONGS TO:

_____

For Katie and Zoë

This paperback edition published in 2012 by Andersen Press Ltd.
Published in Australia by Random House Australia Pty.,
Level 3, 100 Pacific Highway, North Sydney, NSW 2060.
First published in Great Britain in 1991 by Andersen Press Ltd.
Text and Illustration copyright © Tony Ross, 1991
The rights of Tony Ross to be identified as the
author and illustrator of this work have been
asserted by him in accordance with the
Copyright, Designs and Patents Act, 1988.
All rights reserved.
Colour separated in Switzerland by Photolitho AG, Zürich.
Printed and bound in Singapore by Tien Wah Press.

10   9   8   7   6   5   4   3   2   1

British Library Cataloguing in Publication Data available.
ISBN 978 1 84939 355 3
This book has been printed on acid-free paper

A FAIRY Tale

TONY ROSS

ANDERSEN PRESS

THE CLOCK on the mill reflected four o'clock on the shiny roofs of Balaclava Street.

Over an hour to tea, and Bessie was bored. Her book was silly, it was about fairies.

"Fairies! They'd have more sense than to live round here," she thought, staring at the gloomy street outside. "Why can't books be about *real* things instead of made up things all the time?" Outside, the rain was easing, as a yellowy light tickled the black clouds. A long way off, a bird began to sing.

B‌ESSIE went out into the yard and started to bounce a ball. Higher and higher, then too high altogether. The ball disappeared over the wall. Scrambling onto the bin, Bessie peeped over the wall.

Next door's yard was just like her own, except everything was the other way round. Bessie clambered over. It didn't feel right, like going into a foreign country. Suddenly, an old lady opened the back door. Bessie went white, and began to explain about the ball. The old lady smiled, and asked when Bessie's mother got home.

"Ten past five, please, Miss."

"Come in for a while then," smiled the old lady.

"My name's Mrs Leaf, and I know you're Bessie."

As they sat down to buttered bread and tea, Bessie wondered how she knew her name. Then she explained about her silly books.

"So you don't believe in fairies?"

"No!" said Bessie. "There's no such things as magic."

"Prove it," said Mrs Leaf.

Bessie giggled. "You can't prove it. *You* prove there *is*."

Mrs Leaf settled back. "Have you ever had a magic moment?" she said. "A summer afternoon when the sky's so warm the world stops, or the night before Christmas when you can *feel* the happiness in the air?"

" 'course," breathed Bessie.

"There you are then!" laughed Mrs Leaf. "Never pooh-pooh what you don't understand . . . Why, even I might be a fairy."

As THE NEXT DAY was Saturday, Bessie was given a penny to spend, and she went round to Leach's shop to buy some liquorice. Mrs Leaf was there, chatting over the counter, so the two of them walked home together.

"You were funny when you said you were a *fairy*," giggled Bessie.

"Why?" asked Mrs Leaf.

"Well, fairies are little, and pretty," said Bessie.

"They can be," muttered the old lady. "Then again, they can look old and ugly. It all depends on how they feel. When they're sad they can look *awful*, yet when they are happy, they become so dainty they almost float through the air."

"If you really were a fairy then," said Bessie, "you'd be a very sad one." As if to make up for her rudeness, she added quickly, "Can we meet again tomorrow?"

"Of course," smiled Mrs Leaf, closing her front door.

"I'M GOING to pretend you're a fairy," said Bessie. They were walking down by the cut. "Why do you live in a dirty old town like this?"

"I've always lived here," said Mrs Leaf sadly. "You see, fairyworld is right here now, only, you can't see it." She took a coin out of her bag. "It's like you live on one side of this penny, and they live on the other. You're both there, but each can't see t'other."

They stopped by the lock, and Mrs Leaf pointed to the ground. "Fairies don't build anything, so in their world, there's grass right now where those cobbles are." They walked on. "Sometimes a fairy can slip into your world, and if you are very lucky you can see one. Only for an instant though, and only out of the corner of your eye. Perhaps one day I slipped through, and couldn't find a way back."

"Go on!" laughed Bessie. Mrs Leaf chuckled.

A T SCHOOL, Bessie asked her friends if they believed in fairies. In no time at all, she was the joke of the playground.

Of course no one believed in fairies. The *very* idea! With tears in her eyes, Bessie tried to avoid the other children, but it was impossible. They followed her everywhere, jumping about and laughing. After school, they even followed her home, across the croft to Balaclava Street.

Wilfred Gosling flapped his arms, as if he was flying, and Edna Lord pretended to be a Christmas tree fairy. With a lump rising in her throat, Bessie rushed into her house, and slammed the door shut.

Why *couldn't* she believe what she wanted?

Why *couldn't* she ask what she wanted to know?

THAT EVENING, she climbed up onto the moor above the town. From where she sat, she could see the roof of her house. She needed to think things out. She knew there were no fairies, because when her tooth came out, her mother told her to put it under her pillow and the tooth fairy would buy it. Sure enough, there was sixpence the following morning, but Bessie knew it wasn't left by a fairy, because later on, she found her tooth wrapped in tissue, in her mother's treasure box.

But then, Mrs Leaf was not like other old ladies. She didn't get tired for one thing. For another, she ate the queerest stuff. Tea and bread like anyone else, although she always used rainwater for tea, never tap water. She liked lots of lettuce and cucumber, never any meat, and everything was cold.

In fact, she didn't have an oven in her kitchen. Sometimes, she just picked wild berries off the bushes.

"YOU MUST NEVER eat wild berries," she had warned Bessie. "That's elfin food. You would get very ill if you did, just as fairies would get sick if they were to try to eat sweets." Bessie promised never to.

She went home by way of her uncle's house. She met him coming back from work, and after he'd washed and changed, he went to feed his pigeons.

"There ain't no such thing as fairies, is there uncle Harold?" she asked.

"Don't rightly know, Chuck," he said. "I've never seen one, but then I've never seen a pigeon look at a map, but they always gets home all right."

As she trudged home through the twilight, Bessie muttered to herself, "He didn't actually say there *wasn't*. Edna Lord doesn't know everything."

As the weeks turned to months, a strong friendship grew between Bessie and old Mrs Leaf.

O N WHIT MONDAY, the old lady was there to clap as Bessie walked past in the Sunday School Walk. It was so hot that the tar stuck to the soles of Bessie's new shoes. After the special tea in the church hall, the two friends walked home together. They talked of the lovely day, and Bessie wished it would go on forever. "If you *were* a fairy, you could *magic* it to go on forever," she said. "Bless us, no I couldn't," beamed Mrs Leaf. "Fairies have no more magic than you do."

"What about the way they change from ugly to pretty then?" said Bessie quickly.

"That's not magic, that's just the way they're made," said Mrs Leaf. "They think you big people are magic."

"*Us!*" gasped Bessie. "*Why?*"

"Well, you start life little, and get bigger, no matter how you feel. That's magic to them. You see, it's only because they don't understand you."

As the months turned to years, Bessie left school, and started work at the mill. Mrs Leaf was still her best friend, although, now Bessie was grown up, she called her by her first name . . . Daisy. Only now and again they talked of the old days, and how Daisy used to try and make Bess believe in fairies.

"Funny thing is," Bess thought, "Daisy doesn't look a day older than when I first met her. Younger in fact . . ."

Then Bess met Robert. He worked at the mill too, although not on a machine. He was in the main office.

Robert took to Daisy straight away, and often said how like sisters she and Bess looked. In the spring, Bess and Robert were married, and they moved into Bess's old house in Balaclava Street. Funny thing about the wedding though, Daisy did not appear on any of the photographs. Sometimes there was a smudge where she should have been.

Robert laughed about that, and said that something always went wrong with the photographs if he had anything to do with it. The three of them had some wonderful times together. That summer, they even went to the seaside together. Daisy became almost like one of the family.

AFTER SIX HAPPY YEARS, it was announced on the wireless that
war had broken out. Robert joined the army straight away.
Bess didn't want him to, but he said it was only right and proper.
There were tears at the station when Robert went off to London
in his new uniform, and he promised to write. Bess was glad that
Daisy was there to see her home, she felt lost without Robert.
In the following months, lots of letters arrived, some from across
the sea. Then, suddenly they stopped, and news came through that
Robert would never come back. A medal came through the post
with Robert's name on it, but it didn't help. Bess was heartbroken,
and Daisy looked after her every day.
As the years rolled by, the sadness about Robert turned into happy
memories, just as Daisy said it would.

As Bess grew older, Daisy just seemed to grow younger. One Christmas night, Bess took a sly glance at her friend, and couldn't help thinking how much nicer she was than the girl on the television show they were watching.

They still walk arm in arm along Balaclava Street, just like an old lady and a little girl of many years ago. It never occurs to Bess how pretty Daisy looks. Maybe old friends never notice the changes in each other.

Now and again though, a faint memory comes to old Bess. Something about fairies looking young and beautiful when they're happy . . . stuff and nonsense, she knew there were no such things . . .

. . . she's always known.

Other books illustrated by
TONY ROSS:

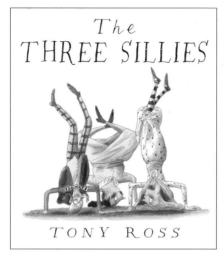

9781849392297

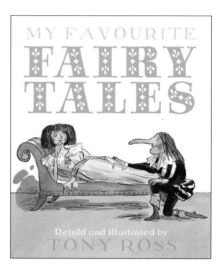

9781849392112

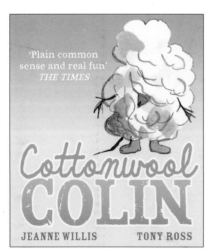

9781842707197

9781842704264

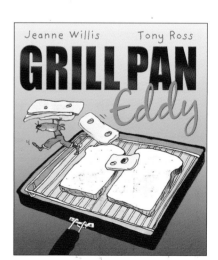

9781842707111